MORALS

Also in the Series

Fartin' Martin Sidebottom is a boy who can't stop breaking wind -
and joins a brass band conducted by The Devil.

Nose-picker Nicholas Pickering can't stop picking his nose -
and ends up inside his own nose and having a terrifying confrontation with The Bogeyman.

Grubby Joe Grub refuses to get washed -
and turns into a dirty pig. He's taken off to the abattoir, only to be saved in the nick of time.

Scary Hairy Mary is a warning to anyone who doesn't brush their hair -
poor Mary gets lost in a frightening jungle.

Messy Bessie Clutterbuck won't keep her bedroom tidy -
and finds herself in the biggest mess of her life at Devil's Dump.

Chilly Billy Winters refuses to wrap up warm -
and is abducted by a gang of zombie snowmen.

Gobby Nobby Robinson can't stop talking -
and is caught in a deadly mouth-trap.

Smelly Simon Smedley won't change his socks -
So Bigfoot pays a visit.

Black-toothed Ruth Black never brushes her teeth -
and gets carried Aberdeenshire tooth devils.

ISBN - 978-1-908211-20-0

A catalogue record for this book is available from the British Library.

First Published in Great Britain in 2014 by Pro-actif Communications
Cameron House, 42 Swinburne Road, Darlington, Co Durham DL3 7TD
Email: books@carpetbombingculture.co.uk
Pro-actif Communications

www.monstrousmorals.co.uk

Bridget Wrigglesworth

If you've got ants in your pants, and you can't sit still,
don't be surprised if your life goes downhill.

There was never a child
who was quite such a fidget,
As my little sister -
our folks named her Bridget.
From the very beginning,
She made Mother ill,
You see, inside the womb,
She just couldn't keep still.

You can ask any mum,
giving birth isn't easy,
Having a baby
can make you feel queasy.
When it starts
tossing and turning
and gives you a kick,
You need a large bucket
to collect all the sick.

Every morning at school when he took registration,
Bridget's teacher was struck by a sense of frustration.
Mr Keating would stop with a glare and a sigh,
As Miss Wrigglesworth's antics in class caught his eye.

In the end, Father took her to see Great Aunt Rose,
whatever the question, she's the lady who knows.
Rose told her: "The reason you wriggle and dance,
"Is down to the fact you've got ants in your pants!"

Later that night, Bridget struggled to sleep,
She closed her eyes tight and tried counting sheep.
But sheep weren't the creatures she saw in her head,
A posse of ants had come crawling instead.

Bridget opened her eyes
and ran for the door,
As insects emerged
from her underwear drawer.
The ants stood in line
at the side of the bed,
There was one with a pair
of pink pants on his head.

These weren't like ants she'd encountered before,
Crawling around on our dining room floor.
These evil ants stood in hostile defiance,
Simply enormous, I swear they were gi-ants.

Bridget's blood turned to ice,
her knees went all weak,
The largest ant coughed
and started to speak:
"We're ants on a mission,
being nasty's our job,
You must have heard tales
of the famed Anthill Mob?"

Bridget was cornered,
there was nowhere to hide,
She was carried away,
down the stairs, then outside.
She shouted and screamed
as loud as she could,
As they marched out of
town and came to a wood.

AAAARRRGGGHHHH!

Deep in the forest they came to a standstill,
There, in a clearing - the world's largest anthill.
Bridget put up a struggle for all she was worth,
But was carried inside the mountain of earth.

The ants weren't the type
to be messing around,
Deeper and deeper,
they went into the mound.
Through endless tunnels,
ever onwards they ploughed,
Til they came to a chamber
where everyone bowed.

Perched high on a throne and devouring a feast,
was a really fat ant weighing six stones at least.
It was hard to believe what big portions she ate:
This was the Queen Ant - Rosemary The Great.

Bridget started to shiver, she broke out in a sweat,
For she couldn't help thinking they'd already met.
There was something familiar - round the eyes and the nose,
Then it struck her - the Queen Ant resembled Aunt Rose!

The more Bridget looked, the more sure she became,
The Queen Ant and Great Aunt were one and the same.
The same pompous look, the same wrinkled skin,
The same chubby face, the same double chin.

The Queen started to talk,
looking down with a sneer:
"Who is that girl-
and why is she here?"
"Bridget's her name, Ma'am,"
a gi-ant explained.
"She has ants in her pants -
it's time she was trained."

From that moment on, Bridget's servant routine,
was fetching and carrying food for the Queen.
With cannonball berries and apples like boulders,
Bridget had more than enough on her shoulders.

All day and all night, she was given no rest,
She was breathless, exhausted, and deeply depressed.
But her fidgeting stopped which I guess goes to prove...
If you work hard enough, you'll be too tired to move.

Most of her captors were mean and sadistic,
Quite anti-social and antagonistic.
But she'd noticed two ants who weren't like the others,
They were either best mates or possibly brothers.

They chatted away as they marched back and forth,
In high, squeaky accents - from somewhere up north.
Each time they passed Bridget, they gave her a smile,
The friendliest insects she'd seen by a mile.

They met her in secret,
away from the crowd,
When they had to go back,
the taller one vowed:
"Don't fret bonny lass,
we'll be back in tick,
My name is Ant...
and they call my mate Dick."

UNUSED TUNNEL

From that moment on,
Ant and Dick both agreed,
They would do what they could
to get Bridget freed.
One night after work,
while the other ants snoozed,
They went to a tunnel
that no one else used.

"You must run," whispered Ant,
"this is your chance!"
So Bridget, the girl who had
ants in her pants,
Ran through the darkness,
just like Ant said,
Til a small speck of light
could be seen straight ahead.

She ran like the wind
but she slipped and then stumbled,
As a noise in the distance
echoed and rumbled.
The floor of the tunnel
had started to shake,
The alarm had been sounded -
the ants were awake.

The beat from their feet, like a rhythmical drumming,
Grew louder and louder - an ant army was coming.
Bridget gave it her all but it wasn't enough,
The ants were upon her and she'd run out of puff.

After all she'd been through,
she was bound to be caught,
Smothered by ants -
what a horrible thought.
Bridget fell to her knees,
defeated and crying...
But the very next moment
she was in the air flying.

A voice in her ear said she wasn't alone,
"Don't worry, Bridget, we'll soon have you home."
Ant and Dick had grown wings, they were rare flying ants,
That's how they saved Bridget - by the seat of her pants.

Now, Mr Keating never gives her black looks,
I can honestly say she's in his good books.
She doesn't dare fidget - too frightened, I think,
In fact, it's been months since she even dared blink.

And the Monstrous Moral of this story...
don't fidget in class - or your life will be PANTS!